Can You Hear the Sea?

First published in Great Britain in 2006 by
Bloomsbury Publishing Plc,
36 Soho Square,
London, W1D 3QY

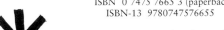

ISBN 0 7475 7657 2 (hardback)
ISBN-13 9780747576570

ISBN 0 7475 7665 3 (paperback)
ISBN-13 9780747576655

Printed in China by South China Printing Co.

1 3 5 7 9 10 8 6 4 2

All papers used by Bloomsbury Publishing are
natural, recyclable products made from wood
grown in well-managed forests. The manufacturing
processes conform to the environmental regulations
of the country of origin

Designed by **Tribal Design Partnership**

Judy Cumberbatch

Can You Hear the Sea?

Pictures by
Ken Wilson-Max

BLOOMSBURY
CHILDREN'S
BOOKS

❋ *On Saturday* ❋

Sarah's grandpa went to the big town.
Before he left, he gave Sarah a shell.
Pink and orange and green,
the loveliest shell she had ever seen.

'It's a magic shell,' said Grandpa.
'If you listen carefully,
you'll hear the sea.'

'Will I really?'
asked Sarah.

'Oh, yes,'
said Grandpa.

'*Don't* go believing
all that nonsense,' said Grandma,
as she plaited Sarah's hair.

But Sarah didn't listen.
Grandpa knew about everything.
He could tell the time by the sun,
knew when the rains would come,
and never, never, ever told a lie.

✳ *On Sunday* ✳

Sarah put the shell to
her ear and listened on
the way to church. But
all she heard was . . .

. . . Rev'rend
William Johnson
praying,

Kofi playing the
drums and singing,

and Grandma humming.

◉ *On Monday* ◉

Sarah listened to her shell
by the river as she and
Grandma did the washing.
But what she heard was . . .

. . . water splashing,

Grandma
beating out
the sheets and
thumping,

and the clothes
flip-flapping.

❈ *On Tuesday* ❈

It was market day.
Sarah listened to her shell as
she walked between
the stalls. But what
she heard was . . .

. . . Mr Victor's
sewing machine
click-clacking,

Mrs Nansi's
tongue yak-yakking,

and the market
mammies haggling
all day long.

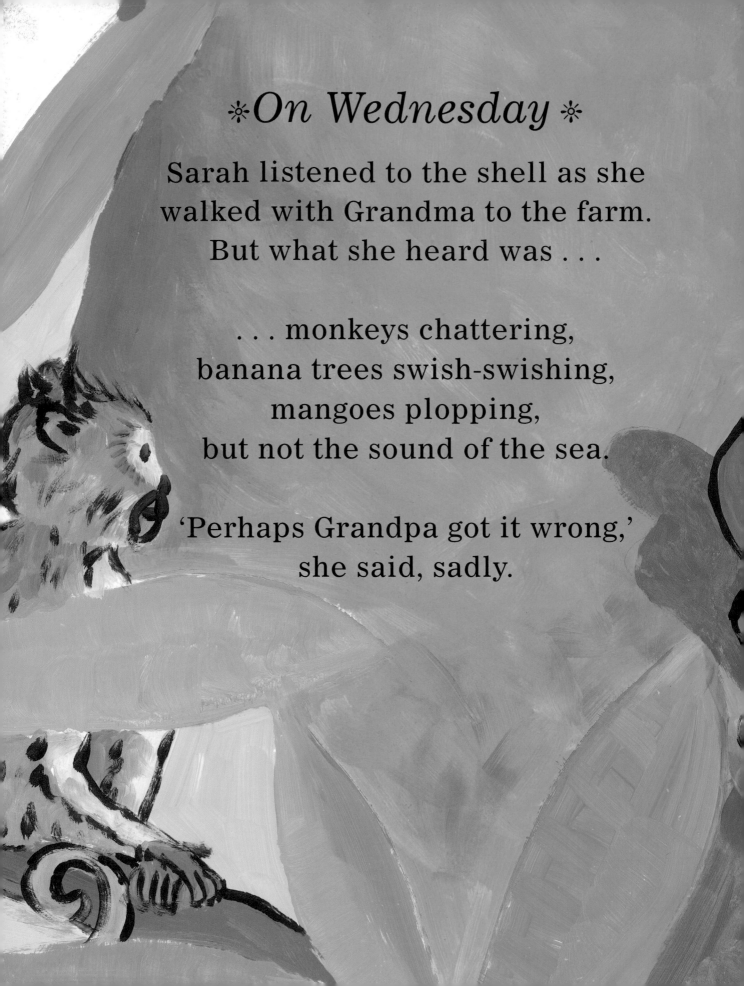

✳ On Wednesday ✳

Sarah listened to the shell as she
walked with Grandma to the farm.
But what she heard was . . .

. . . monkeys chattering,
banana trees swish-swishing,
mangoes plopping,
but not the sound of the sea.

'Perhaps Grandpa got it wrong,'
she said, sadly.

❋ On Thursday ❋

Grandma turned the whole house upside down, and Sarah was busy all day long with the sweeping and the cleaning.

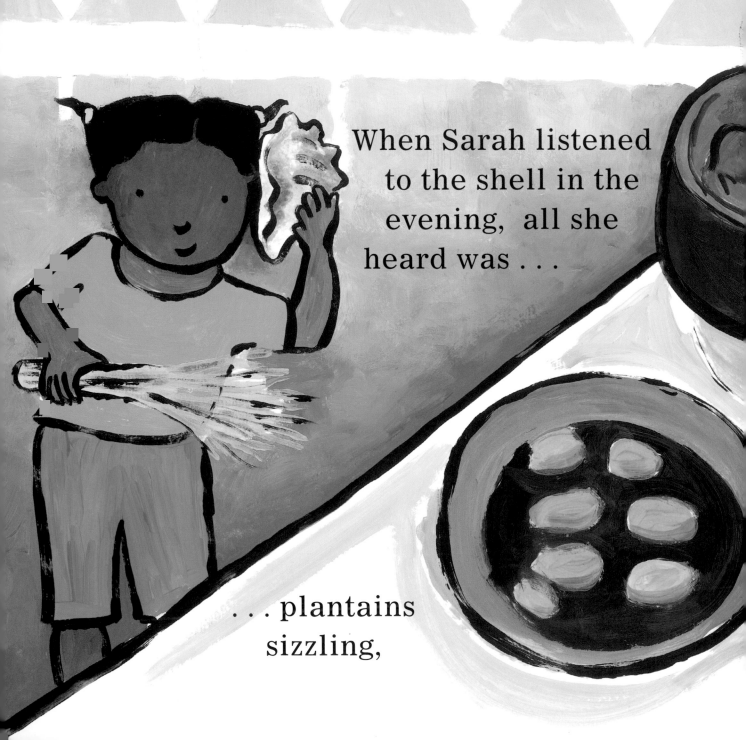

When Sarah listened to the shell in the evening, all she heard was . . .

. . . plantains sizzling,

pepper stew
sput-sputtering,

and Grandma
snoring.

✳ *On Friday* ✳

Sarah went to meet Grandpa.
The tro-tro taxis tooted, water
sellers shouted, buses hooted,
and Grandpa came.

'That's some silly shell,'
she told him.
'I've listened and listened
and heard everything
but the sea.'

✳ *On Saturday* ✳

Grandpa and Sarah sat under the mango tree. Sarah held the shell to her ear.

'Tell me what you hear,'
Grandpa said.

Sarah listened.

'Boys playing football,'
she said.

'Listen,' said Grandpa.

'Next door neighbour's
baby's screaming!'
cried Sarah.

'I can't hear the sea!'

'Quiet,' said Grandpa. 'Now, close your eyes, and this time listen to what the shell tells.'

Sarah put the shell to her ear, closed her eyes, and listened. At first, all she could hear was Grandpa's breathing.

Then, louder and louder, as she listened, came

the sound of

water crashing,

waves pounding,

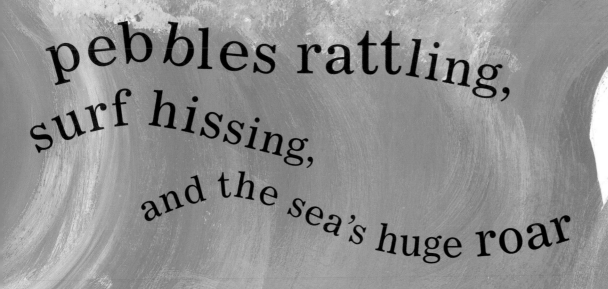

pebbles rattling,
surf hissing,
and the sea's huge roar
on the wide seashore.

'I can hear it,' Sarah said.
'I can hear the sea.'

'Didn't I tell you,' said Grandpa, smiling.